TABOO EROTICA BUNDLE

SLAVES OF SEX

4-IN-1 BOXED SET

GIDEON ELLIOT

WARNING

This book contains sexually explicit scenes and adult language. It may be considered offensive to some readers. This book is for sale to adults ONLY.

Please store your files wisely where they cannot be accessed by underage readers.

* * * * * * * * * * * * * * * * * * *

WANT FREE COPIES OF MY BOOKS?
Just visit my blog and download free copies of my books:
http://gideon-elliot.awesomeauthors.org/gideon-elliot/

About the Publisher

4Fun Publishing, a member of **BLVNP Incorporated**, 340 S. Lemon #6200, Walnut CA 91789, info@blvnp.com / legal@blvnp.com

NOTE: Due to the highly emotional reaction of some people to works of erotic fiction, any email sent to the above address that contains foul language or religious references is automatically deleted by our anti-spam software and will not be seen. All other communications are welcome.

DISCLAIMER

Slaves of Sex

4-in-1 Boxed Set
Taboo Erotica Bundle

By: Gideon Elliot

© Gideon Elliot 2015
ISBN: 978-1-62761-688-1

TABLE OF CONTENTS

BOOK TITLES

An Empty Landscape

I am a Masochist

La Belle Dame Sans Merci

The Face beneath the Mask

AN EMPTY LANDSCAPE

GIDEON ELLIOT

An Empty Landscape

It often seemed to me that I should greatly prefer a life of adventure, a physically challenging life, an out-of-doors life, to the sedentary one I lived. I was routinely bound to desk work—in the winter, as a graduate candidate for an MBA; during the summer, cooped in a cubicle, a head set over my ears, a microphone covered with a prophylactic foamy hardly an inch away from my mouth, writing orders and taking complaints. I crammed at school and up-sold at work and hardly had time for anything else. Perhaps an occasional beer with Jon at Crazy Benny's, but hardly ever even that.

One of the few nights I did pass at Benny's, a balmy one late in June, I became plaintive about my plight after our third beer, and Jon finally said, "I never realized just how big a fool you are." He was smiling, and naturally, I responded asking him what prompted such an unflattering observation.

"Well," he said, "I didn't know how much you hated what you're doing and…." Typically, I did not let him finish his sentence. "Hate it?" I said. "I can't stand it."

"Instead of whining and camping," he said sternly, "do something about it."

"Like what?" I said defiantly.

"If that's going to be your attitude," he said, "you deserve to get a fat ass, a swollen gut, an empty head and a limp prick sitting in cubicles the rest of your life and dreaming about things you can't let yourself remember you've dreamed about. Maybe every now and then scribbling down a fantasy and thinking you've written a story."

I went home to bed that night drunk enough not to have to think about what he said.

~~oOo~~

In the morning, Joel, one of the guys I shared an apartment with on West 74th Street woke me saying there was a call for me. With a full bladder and a piss hard-on tenting my jockeys I sat up and took the phone.

"Hello."

"Are you ready to jump ship?" It was Jon.

"What the fuck you talking about?"

"Call in sick, today and meet me in an hour at the entrance to the park at Columbus Circle."

"Are you crazy?"

"No, you are. Do as I say." It was a warm morning and the sky was a bright azure. "Ok," I said. "But this better be good."

"Be on time," was all he said and hung up.

1. *"A slave to my life circumstances —but not the same as being enslaved to a Master, to be submissive and devoted. That's one thing. An impossible dream. To be beaten down is something else."*

2. *"Lean, muscular, not bulging; need training and breaking in; need Master to erase mind as is and fill it with Himself. No desire but His, no consciousness but His."*

3. *"I crave loss of identity, obliteration of will. I want to become truly determined by a Master's commands. Slavery is freedom. Submission is assertion."*

4. *"The one essential: To be pleasing. The one desire: To be dominated."*

5. *"Pierced nipples, ringed cock, collared neck, clouded mind, eyes gazing at nothing = devotion; obedience.*

6. *"Reality for a slave is whatever his Master causes slave to believe. Anything else, no matter how 'real,' is false.*

7. *"Bowed in submission,*

8. *"Steddieslave""*

"How the hell did you get that?" I said, aghast that he was reading from my secret notebook.

"You don't deny you wrote it," Jon said.

"What's that to you? How did you get my notebook? Give it back to me." I grabbed for it. He slapped me and I fell backwards but caught myself.

"What the hell are you doing? What's going on?

"Adam, we've known each other, been trusted friends for a long time…and you've been holding back telling me about stuff like this?"

"How did you get this? What gave you the right…," I sputtered.

"Shut up now and listen to me, Stedman, and listen attentively," he said with authority that took my breath away. "Nothing gives me the right. I have it because of who I am. And from now on, you're going to do just what I tell you to do because of who you are. There will be consequences that you won't like, if you fail to. But when I'm finished with you, you're even going to like them."

I quit my job and I dropped out of school. I never got an MBA. I moved into his place and instead of paying rent I served as a houseboy.

~~oOo~~

One evening, as I was starting to prepare his dinner, he said, "I want to go out with you dressed as a woman. Tonight. Forget dinner. We'll go to a restaurant."

He looked at me as if he were figuring me out, trying to see how he wanted me. "I want to see you all in silver," he said. He dressed me in silver-tinted nylon stocking, a silver garter belt, silver lamée panties, and he put silver powder on my nipples. He put a pair of ankle strap high-heel silver slippers on me, kneeling in front of me as he did.

He kissed me, and without letting go of our lips, he took me into the bathroom, sat me in front of a vanity mirror, styled my hair to look like a woman's who was trying for a male cut, made me up with eyeliner, eye shadow, lipstick.

"Look at yourself in the mirror" he said. I did and could hardly believe it.

"Do you see how beautiful you look?"

"Yes, I do," I said.

After I'd slithered into a very tight silver mini-skirt and a midriff-baring, skin-tight, stretch metallic silver t-shirt with tiny epaulet sleeves, he clipped silver disks the size of dimes onto my ear lobes. The streets were teaming with hot bodies looking for excitement.

No matter how much any of the guys looking at me as we walked together excited me, I had to stay completely aloof. It was the object of so much desire and I had to learn to keep myself above it. I had to become comfortable with cruelty. It became an aphrodisiac.

I walked beside him totally concentrated on presenting myself to him, on performing for him: whatever I did, I knew in my solar plexus, that I was doing it for him. I was absolutely enchanting as we walked through the still lighted streets, past the garish store windows, past the couples in love and those who were stuck with each other, could not stand each other and stayed with each other in their private boredom, passed open manholes with yellow fence pipes around them, past loud cars with banging radios and shrieking passengers.

I woke up early the next morning and felt his lips pocketing my cock, his tongue taking me beyond control to the edge of lust, his fingers fanning my nipples. I moaned to let him know I was conscious. He lifted his head.

~~oOo~~

Three years later, he suggested we split up. He said he understood, and that he'd give me some money, but he wanted us to go our separate ways.

I first saw Tom at a distance. He was working, bare-chested, at a construction site on Ninth Avenue not far from where I'd gotten a job. He was sun bronzed and beautifully muscled. I was fascinated to watch the pull and swing of his arms and torso as he worked with a pick-axe.

It was the first bright image I had enjoyed since Jon had broken up with me. I walked around the city at a loss. I applied at Pinchon and Broadfells to be a stockbroker's clerk, glad to have that rut to fall back into, in exile with a broken heart, but they wouldn't be hiring for at least six months. Things were precarious, so until I'd hear from them, I had taken a job in a diner on Ninth Avenue as a short order cook.

I watched him. I didn't know his name then. He kept his long tawny blond hair out of his eyes with a red bandana knotted high around his forehead. His chest was honey bronze. His jeans were cut-offs; he wore ankle high work boots and thick gray socks with orange stripes around the top. His legs were bronze like his chest and muscled gracefully like a champion race horse.

I spotted him several times in a straight bar across the street from Crazy Benny's where I used to hang out now and then with some Village poets I'd met wandering around, not friends exactly. They thought macho was hip and didn't want, just because they wrote poetry, to be mistaken for pansies. They didn't know about my past with Jon.

They weren't very good poets, which I pointed out to them when we were all drunk—not first rate, and we had some pretty convoluted arguments. They hated when I told them they'd never write anything approaching worthwhile until they surrendered up their male vanity. I admit it was a waste of time and maybe even a foolish thing to do, but, truth be told, there was one among them I thought was really a sweet guy underneath it, and I was queer for him. I had convinced myself that he could be turned around if I had just the patience. But that's another story. I was trying to be Jon.

Tom was not a part of this group. He was a solitary.

"Buy you a beer?" I said sitting down next to him.

"Sure," he smiled. "What's in it for you?"

"Conversation. Company. Getting to know what life is like for somebody else. Cheers! I banged my stein against his when the beer came. You work construction long?"

"How'd you know I work construction?"

"I've often seen you on Twenty-seventh Street."

"Yeah, well, it's only temporary."

"What's permanent?"

"I'm afraid nothing's permanent."

"That's the second cynical thing you've said in the space of less than a minute."

"Yeah. Hey I'm sorry. I don't mean to be. It's just the way it is. I should go home. I have to get up in the morning. And my neck is sore."

He was actually whining. The discrepancy floored me.

"I know about cynicism," I said. "Go ahead, complain."

I began massaging his neck.

That feels good he said, moving his body away from my hands.

"I got to go."

"I'll walk with you," I said. And we left.

He was tall, well built. His jeans fit nicely. His skimpy t-shirt showed his muscles. He wore knee-high boots over his jeans. I was worshipping him in my mind. I wanted it to be real, too. But I had a sense he wouldn't let on he knew what I was talking about if I told him.

He was cold, indifferent, self-absorbed and unavailable. That made him all the more desirable to me.

"I gotta get up in the morning, and this is where I live. Good night." He extended his hand. I shook it. He was gone.

~~oOo~~

I worked in the diner till eleven most nights, and then I'd trek south past the meat market and onto Christopher to try my luck.

As he stepped out from between two trucks, I saw him, and a fire began to burn in my bones. He approached and took hold of me by the eyes. He offered me a joint.

"On the street?"

"On the street."

"But…"

"There's nothing to be afraid of when you do what I say." I inhaled and handed him back the joint.

"How are you called?"

"You mean my name?"

"How are you called, boy? I'm not in the habit of saying things twice."

"Boy," I said.

"Boy," he repeated.

"Call me Sir," he said.

"Sir," I said.

"What do you do?"

"I'm a stockbroker's clerk. I'm going for my license." I'd gotten the news that afternoon I'd gotten a job on Wall Street, and I'd given notice at the diner.

"Do you like your work?"

"No, Sir."

"I'm a collector. I collect boys like you and keep them here, until...." he indicated the end of his sentence with a wave of his hand. "I want you to be a part of my collection. I'll take good care of you." He took hold of me, kissed me, breathed his smoky breath into my mouth. I swallowed him. I was dizzy and rigid with excitement. My whole body felt like it was made of marble. I had not been this way since living with Jon. He took me round the shoulders and we walked down Hudson until we came to an old brownstone.

"This is where I live," he said, opening an old oak door with a frosted art nouveau window into the front hall, "and where I have my gallery, where I keep my boys and display them." He led me upstairs. I was happy to let myself be led.

End of the 1ˢᵗ Book

I AM A
MASOCHIST

GIDEON ELLIOT

I am a Masochist

The moon was in the center of the sky. My heart was light. My head was clear. The hedges were bursting with green, vital, newly emerged leaves. The street was quiet and empty. A shiver of danger shot through the nocturnal euphoria.

At the corner, he was leaning against the lamppost, cigarette hanging from his lips, hair slicked back at the sides and falling in curls over his forehead; two admiring lieutenants flanked him, copies of him in dress and stance, but far from his equals in arrogant and graceful power. That was only his. They knew they lacked it, and they willingly subordinated themselves to him just to be near it.

"Hey, you," he said, "you going somewhere." I felt the threat and ignored it.

"I'm talking to you," he said in a soft and threatening voice. He didn't let it go. He didn't let me pass. His lieutenants were on either side of me, each seizing an arm before I knew it.

Usually, there's a little hassle, minor roughing up and major humiliation. You leave one of these encounters feeling like shit. But this was different. One of them put a handkerchief over my mouth and nose, and I passed out.

I was dazed when I awoke, and out of it. I knew what was going on as if I were seeing everything from a distance, myself included. But I was indifferent. Feeling no pain. I was naked. My hands were cuffed together around a high bar suspended over me and my feet just touched the floor. He was examining me.

"Scared?" The question was threatening and ironic at the same time. I was unable to answer. It was only when I felt him making a fist around my cock that I realized it was hard. My whole body stiffened with anxiety. Then he took my ball sac in his palm, closed it around me and squeezed hard. I gasped at first and he slapped me with his other hand, simultaneously increasing the pressure on my scrotum. I passed out. I came to on the street. It was dawn. I lifted myself, felt in my pockets. Nothing had been taken from me, not my keys, not my wallet, not my phone.

~~oOo~~

I was sitting in the Café Figaro drinking espresso and reading Rilke. It was a rainy Tuesday afternoon, three days later. I'd gone to my morning classes, but had trouble focusing and decided the afternoon would be better spent not trying to. Rilke kept fading away and my mind seemed to evaporate. I was overcome by the memory of his hand around my cock. I was getting hard under the table.

It was dark by the time I left, and for no good reason I walked over to Sheridan Square and then over to Hudson Street. There was a building I would have said I'd never been in, but I walked up to it and rang one of the bells. A buzzer sounded in response and I pushed the door open and walked over to the elevator like I knew where it was. I pressed seven and got off inside a loft.

I was very relaxed. It was warm. I had to get out of my shirt. I'd feel so much more comfortable without it. My chest was filling with breath. Slowly I took my shirt off.

He took hold of my nipples. I felt myself levitate. Something curled itself around me. But it's like a dream I can't remember.

~~oOo~~

I didn't go to a barber to get my hair cut. I let it grow. From time to time, I twisted this way and that in front of a mirror and took a handful of hair at the back or on the sides and cut it off. I was shaggy. Likewise, I was careless about how I dressed and what I ate. I was a little fat, and I was altogether flabby. It didn't matter much to me.

I spent a lot of time doing research in the library and even more in front of my computer. My work was in demand. Money was not a problem. I had enough in several bank accounts that I could have stopped working and going to school and lived ok for a long time. But I liked work. It filled up my time. And I was looking to meet somebody at school.

At the same time, I was pretty much a loner. Meeting someone would be nice. But I was worried that it might be too much trouble if I did. I was afraid of the demands someone I got involved with would saddle me with. I could take care of myself.

I was surprised to find myself sitting in a barber chair, a sheet tied round my neck, getting my hair cut. Sal – how did I know his name? -- scolded me.

"Who cuts your hair?"

"I do it myself."

"It shows. No more. You come to me. Today is just a start. I give you a chance to grow something good-looking. What you got now, it looks…" He didn't finish the sentence, but the look on his face of disdain mingled with disgust said more than I wanted to hear. I hardly recognized myself when he got finished. A lot of hair was on the floor.

"Better," Sal said.

It was hard for me to agree with him. But, it really did feel good to have my head shaved. I felt like I was getting a hard on, paid up and gave a tip and got out of there before I could be even more embarrassed, but not before Sal made me promise to come back in a month for a real hair cut.

"We gonna make you worth it."

I couldn't figure out what that meant.

I wandered around the Village the rest of the day. I was restless. On the corner, where Sheridan Square feeds into Christopher Street, on one side, and West 10th on the other, through a large double window up above me, on the second floor, I saw guys working out. I didn't go to a gym. I wasn't into body-building.

Today, I felt like seeing what was going on inside, anyhow. A cool guy at the desk said I could go the first time free, see if I liked it and then join up if I wanted. He asked me if I needed some gym clothes since it didn't look like I had my own.

I never thought I could get so much pleasure working out. An hour became two and two nearly three. I was actually surprised at my own stamina and strength.

I registered with Mike at the desk and wrote a check. "Welcome," he said. He was looking at my shaved skull. "I like it," he said. "Thanks," I smiled.

~~oOo~~

The evening was dreary and felt darker than usual. The Seventh Avenue tar was slick from the rain, and the red and yellow echoes of neon signs and stoplights slithered, shimmering, across the surface. I'd had a headache all day. A workout was essential.

"Hey," Mike said when I entered the gym. "Tough day."

"You're sharp."

"Come here." I walked over to the desk. "Get out of your clothes and go into the massage room. I'll give you a rub down before you work out." He said it with his large warm hand grasping my shoulder.

"Thanks," I said.

In three months of working out daily, my body had undergone a terrific change. So had I. I'd greatly reduced the hours I spent working in front of the computer, but what I did with the time was hard to figure out. It was like a daydream I kept going in and out of.

I wasn't stripped and spread on the table long when Mike walked in. He put his palm on my lower back and cupped the back of my neck with his other hand.

"Relax, he said, and I did, immediately, automatically. I rose from unfathomable depth and danced to the music of his touch.

I often returned to the loft on Hudson Street and I never was sure how I had gotten there, but I knew it was the place I was supposed to be, that the place that was real, that the rest of my life was an illusion, that the man there was my superior and that I had tom that I wanted to obey him. I was sensitive to his commands and I anticipated what he wished for me.

I was nourished by his praise, and I was grateful when he chastised me, disciplined me, punished me. I needed him. I was proud to wear his black leather uniform. I treasured the times he allowed me to worship him, when he permitted me to tongue his instep and worship at his ankles; then my whole body was as hard as my cock.

I could not understand why my classmates were alarmed, concerned, confused. They told me I looked different, that I acted strange, that I was not "myself," that I dressed and spoke in an unfamiliar way. I did not know what they were talking about. This freaked them out even more: that I could look blankly at them with not the least sign of recognition. They said it made them feel like they were crazy or like I was one of the pod people.

My only response was to smile, throw my arm around the guy if he was the least bit good looking and say, "enough of this crap; what are you doing later this afternoon?"

A surprising number said "nothing" and were pleased to spend the afternoon with me. I could tell I excited them, and I never had trouble getting their clothes off and our cocks out.

It was strange how many began telling me that they were in love with me and hated the time they couldn't spend with me. It left me cold and I turned off before their eyes, but the farther away I got the crazier about me they became.

There was a particularly sweet, dark-haired boy who effected me differently. With him I did not become cold and distant. I had a great big school-girl, vanilla crush on him. We spent hours walking in the park, sitting on the benches and frisking with each other. I felt a desire for him that frightened me. Gently, I kissed him on the lips; tenderly, I swept the tips of my fingers over the tips of his nipples. They stiffened and ripples of laughter spilled over his face.

He looked at me with pleading eyes. I was his last hope. I lost myself with him in some early nineteenth century fantasy, and romance was our master. And by that I was blaspheming, for I had begun to value this adorable boy more than my real master. Even in his presence, even when he swung the blue crystal with the glowing gleam of a ruby in its center before my eyes and instructed me to follow its movement back and forth, my mind wandered, my eyes wished to rest not on oblivion but on my beloved.

You would not believe I was such a fool as not to imagine that my master would notice this. But I was so transported. I had no mind to give it. He locked my cock against my scrotum with a ring anchored at its base. I could not extend myself sexually, but I could befoul myself with a urinary leak when pressed, and rinse myself off with embarrassment.

And the boy, suddenly, was not the person I thought he'd been. I was in this crippled state neither of use nor interest to him. I could not feel anger at him, although I was stung by his new coldness, but held myself accountable and felt my own unworthiness, my clumsiness. There was something in me which craved domination and that was going to mess things up. It was inevitable. I could not blame him.

I know it's a cliché, but his beauty blazed as he walked out the door. From his throne in my heart, my master was laughing.

End of the 2nd Book

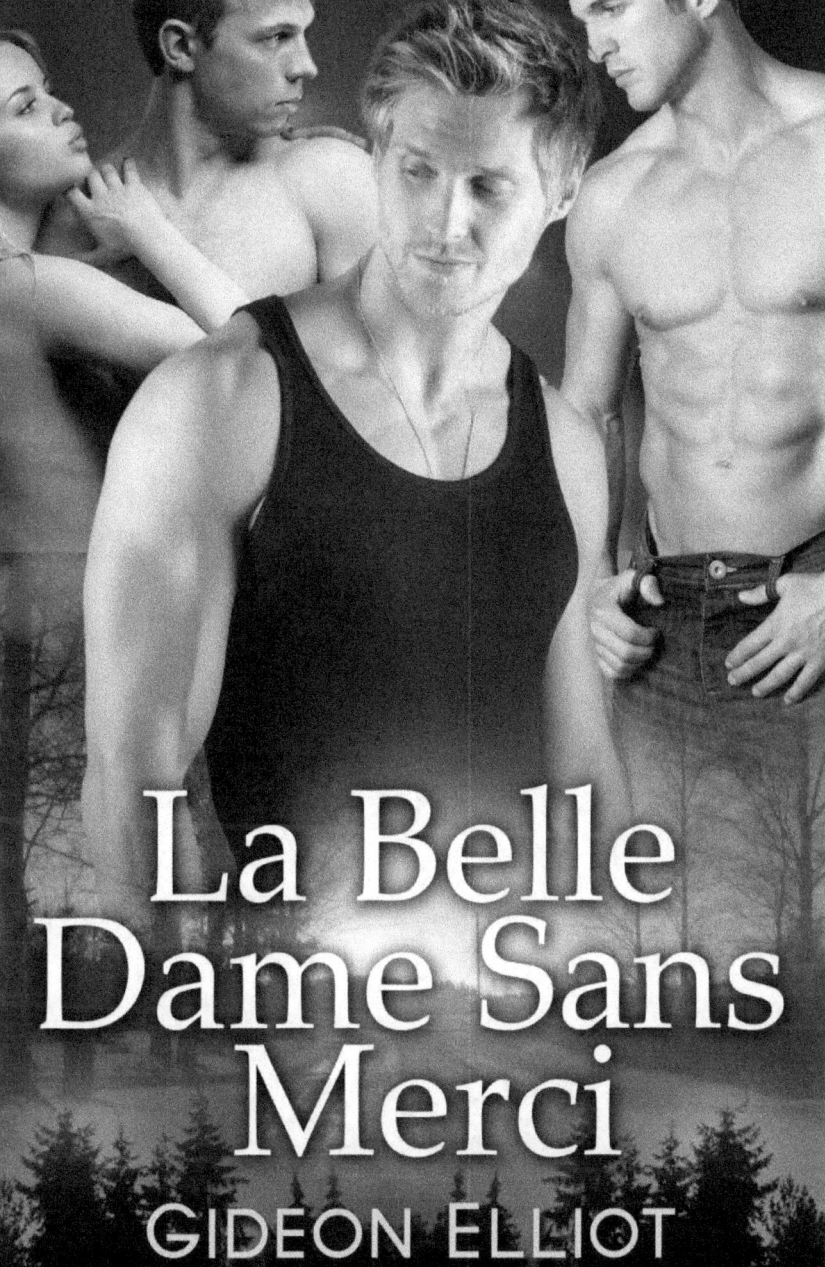

La Belle Dame Sans Merci

GIDEON ELLIOT

La Belle Dame Sans Merci

Although it was already the end of June, winds like those in March howled. The banging of the front gate startled Matthew awake. He raised his head from his desk. He had fallen asleep on his book, like a schoolboy during a classroom rest period. He got up and went out through the back door to the garden. A mist was sweating out from the cloud that had settled on the hillside. Summer was slow to come this year and the air was chilly as well as damp. He was glad there was enough wood left in the cellar from the winter to make a proper fire this night.

He passed through the rattling gate and walked along the roadside, holding his jacket close over his chest and peering down the distance for some sign of headlights that did not appear. He fastened the gate, went back into the house, brought logs up from the cellar, built a fire, made it roar.

Daphne was jealous that Ronald was seeing Matthew, and she became panicked when she saw his overnight bag near the door.

"I'm going now," Ronald said to her. She stood frozen showing hurt and anger. "I'll be back in two weeks." She frowned.

"This is important."

"You'll sleep with him."

"I'm going there to work."

She looked at him defiantly disbelieving.

"I'm his editor."

"So edit, for chrissake."

"Daphne, I don't want to leave you when you're like this," Ronald said. On the other hand, and this he did not say, although he knew she knew it anyhow, he did not want to be with her when she was like this, either. "I understand this is difficult," he said.

"Don't talk about understanding. If you understood, you wouldn't do this."

"That's not fair."

"You're talking about fairness."

"If you try to bind me to you, it won't be me that's bound to you but a beaten man, and to him you won't want to be bound."

"You can do it because you don't have feelings. You have words. That's all everything you say is, only words. There's no heart. There's no connection, Ronald. No feelings! Just words, words, words!"

By this time she was screaming at him, and he was paralyzed by the force of her demand. She was challenging him to be cruel. That's the only way he could see to get what he wanted. Doing what he wanted and being cruel had become—she had made them so—identical.

"At least, stay until morning. Then go," she said begging, bargaining. "I won't make a fuss then. I promise."

He capitulated. "But I have to telephone Matthew not to wait for me tonight."

"No," she said, blurting it out and pulling it back simultaneously.

Ronald looked at her, and Daphne sensed the anger about to flare and quickly put her hands on his chest. "I don't want to share you tonight. I want all of you. I know what happens when you talk to him." She gave a wicked nip to his earlobe.

But when she lay with him later in bed, he did not touch her, and no effort of hers succeeded in exciting him or pulling him out of himself. He lay, hands cupped under his head, staring at the ceiling until, at last, he fell asleep. She felt sorry for him, and circled her hand on his strong chest as he slept; she was overwhelmed by a sense of love. She wanted to do something for him.

So Matthew sat up in Glover, Vermont, not far from where the Bread and Puppet Theater has its Great Outdoor Amphitheater and Pine Forest, waiting for Ronald, who was not coming, at least not this night. He kept himself busy—he always kept himself busy, feeling there was no justification for being without doing—correcting the galleys for his new book on the role of money, imperialism, and the poverty of culture in devitalizing democracy.

It was about two in the morning, and through the old wavy glass panes of his office windows in the converted barn he saw headlights coming up his driveway. Thinking it was Ronald—Who else could it have been but Ronald? He was expecting Ronald. Had he suspected it to be anyone else but Ronald he would have been frightened.—Matthew jogged down the steps and stepped onto the porch to greet Ronald. The wind had not died down.

Before he could be frightened, as he realized it wasn't Ronald, he saw that whoever it was had a kindness, a gentleness, a tenderness to him, openly broadcast by a face that was not only movie-star handsome but sweet. His long, muscled torso was commanding. He wore a tight-fitting black t-shirt; his jeans were tight, too; his thighs were strong and long; he wore English boots.

"Excuse me, sir," he said. "I saw your lights on, so I got the nerve to intrude." The wind was mussing his hair. "I need to rest for the night. I'd like to ask hospitality from you. Can you provide me with someplace to crash, or at least let me park me and my car here till daybreak? And then I'll be on my way."

"Come inside," Matthew said.

"Thank you." There was not much that needed to be said beyond what their eyes said. Matthew took him to his own bed.

David undressed slowly. Matthew enjoyed looking at him. David smiled at him with his warm green eyes. He peeled his shirt off. Matthew looked at his sleek, slim, smooth, tanned, muscled body, naked now but for a black string bikini, stuffed with his cock. Matthew's gaze rested on David's shoulders, neck, torso, his ridged abs, narrow waist. His eyes burst with desire at the strength and grace and definition of David's ass and thighs. He admired the strength of his legs and found beauty in his ankle bone and long toes. They lay naked beside each other eyes to eyes, breaths intermingling lost in the delight of being hard together, cock to cock.

~~oOo~~

When Ronald arrived the next afternoon—it was after two—he found them in the kitchen wet from the shower with towels around themselves and drinking coffee. Matthew clapped him on the back and his towel fell to the floor when he stretched, but he stayed in the embrace, naked against the fine worsted silk of Ronald's summer suit, a sandy brown three button Versace with pleated pants. It had a golden yellow vertical chalk stripe. Matthew tilted back a little, tugged Ronald to him by the knot of his gold and magenta tie of tiny paisleys swimming on a field of pale green a tone darker than his shirt, and gave his lips a job that made him forget the city.

"You ok?" he asked. "What happened?"

"Daphne..."

"...rose up and railed against the vice of errancy."

"Matthew, put on some clothes."

"First let me introduce you. David, Ronald. Ronald, David. Ronald is an editor who is here to try to make me write another book because, strangely enough, there's money in it. David is a spirit of the landscape that paid a visit to my door last night to remind me that nature is beneficent."

~~oOo~~

Anne's gaze dropped from searching the girders of the globe balanced on the shoulders of the statue of Atlas. Its presence marked the importance of the Fifth Avenue office building before which it stood. Her attention came down to street level when she sensed Daphne was passing. She had seen the girl several times before in the late afternoon, and she couldn't get her out of her mind.

She took in the girl's full form. She was twenty-three and full of smoldering fire that needed blowing to blaze up. She wore a short skirt that showed her legs, good legs, knock-out legs, shapely legs, graceful tapering ankles, thighs you couldn't help wanting to kiss, to caress, to run up and down with your tongue. She pranced, she danced, she swerved, she curved in stockings and heels. She had hips, she had breasts, discrete, but all there, assured. She wore lipstick and eye-make-up and fixed her long tumbling hair in an old-fashioned way that made her adorable.

Anne became so hungry for her, she began to follow her, making an about face and walking north up Fifth Avenue. She punched in Peggy's number as the children's zoo passed on her left and spoke as she walked.

"Hey hon, I'm really sorry, but there's no way I'm gonna make it....I trust your color sense entirely....No, I promise I won't scold...if I don't like the results....You are?...Ok, Kid, let me get off....See you....next Thursday....For sure....For sure for sure....Ciao."

~~oOo~~

David stayed with Matthew and so did Ronald. Rather than the two putting clothes on when Ronald arrived, he took his off. He stiffened when he saw that David reacted to him by becoming hard. The three of them all slept in Matthew's big bed. David caressed Mathew's scrotum as Matthew kissed Ronald with a kiss that went all the way to the back of his throat. Matthew circled his fingers around the nubs of David's tight nipples and David took Matthew's cock deep in his mouth. Ronald's fingers danced on the column of David's cock as if it were a flute or a clarinet.

They were intoxicated with each other (and when Ronald left two weeks later, Matthew had written three sonnet cycles; one long poem; a sestina; and two songs. Ronald had not lied to Daphne. He went back to his office with most of Matthew's next book.)

~~oOo~~

Ronald was glad when he found his place empty and with no sign of Daphne around. She had, in fact, offered to bring Anne there the first time, since the girl Anne shared her apartment with was at home that night. But when she told Anne it was her boyfriend's place, Anne wanted nothing to do with it and said, "I'll take you back to my place, and they got into a cab and headed for Sheridan Square."

Ronald showered after the long trip back, lingering with a soapy finger sliding up and down his anal canal. With his other hand he was caressing his nipples and picturing David's torso. After he ejaculated, he called up Scott Michaelson with the good news that he'd gotten a manuscript out of Matthew and it would be perfect for a deluxe gift edition that could be in the stores in time for Christmas. He read into the phone, picking at random from the manuscript the "Octet":

The heart, grown bitter with disbelief,
Now by this angel presence knows relief.
The eye, pained, seeing nothing it wanted,
Now by images of desire is haunted.
Gift of the night,
Bring me delight.
Body of desire,

In me, burn entire.

~~oOo~~

Anne suspected that despite Daphne's perfect exterior she was less sturdy inside than she appeared as she strode with muscular grace and determination on her high heels through Manhattan streets.

"Come here, Daphne," she said one evening, when they were alone in her place, and Daphne had become her lover. Daphne was standing by the mantle-piece examining Anne's collection of bric-a-brac. She turned, startled by the assertiveness of Anne's tone and stared.

"Come here, Daphne," she repeated with no change in tone. Daphne came to her as if not moving of her own free will but as a magazine model, obeying a command. She stood before her mistress stiffened and trembling. Anne caressed Daphne's abundant hair, tangling it around her fingers like a spider weaving a web with it.

"You really are a bitch."

"Fuck you." Anne said it with a smile.

"No you are," Matthew said. "She's a confused girl and you're confusing her more."

"Where do you come off? I have to admire your arrogance. If there weren't other people in the room, I think I'd hit you."

"You aren't using her?"

"I don't have to analyze, label and define what I do for you, Matthew."

"You're playing with somebody's identity."

"So what's new? What are you doing right now with me?"

"With you?"

"You're playing with my identity. You want to persuade me to be different from what I am."

"There's an obvious difference."

"Yes, you approve of your motives and you disapprove of mine. That's the difference. I mean, what about you and Ronald?" Matthew said nothing. "I suppose that's different too."

"I'm not talking about motives but about effects on a human soul."

"Do you know what the effects are? and who are you to judge them?"

"I know the power of your spells, Anne. You close off the possibility of possibility, of development. You don't let her find her own way out of her problems. You're chaining her to an obsession: longing for you, obedience to you, worshipping you."

"I do believe you're jealous, Mary."

"Now I at least can return your earlier fuck you and reiterate that you are a bitch."

"My barb stung. Hit home, huh?"

"Anne, I wish you would let her loose."

"Matthew, my darling, keep wishing. But I warn you, you haven't seen anything yet."

Even Ronald himself thought he was crazy for not desiring her when he looked at Daphne. A few times—before he really knew her—he could get into her, but then, it disappeared. When she became "a person" to him, she stopped being sexually desirable.

He looked at her, now, as she circled up the steps from the ladies' room back into the large room of the restaurant. She was indeed magnificent, square shoulders, strong collar bones, a neck like ivory and a gait like a gazelle. He would outdo Solomon. But Solomon had him beat by a mile if the number of his wives is any fair indication of the strength of his heterosexual desire.

"What's the matter with you, Ronald that you don't find her attractive?" Anne's question jolted him, for he hadn't said anything about that to her, and here she was just entering into the train of his thought as if it were a conversation with her. Daphne, however, was seating herself before he had time for any response. A stake of fear stuck in his heart. This woman had a dangerous power, and he was uneasy about when or how she might choose to use it.

It was not to be now, however. Anne did not continue what she had started. His fear was mixed with gratitude that she did not proceed to embarrass him, but gracefully she segued into what seemed to be harmless conversation.

Ronald thought to himself, I don't know why Daphne wanted me to meet this woman, but she gives me the willies. I'd never heard Daphne speak of her until recently. And then she became pervasive. Everything Daphne did she referred to Anne: something Anne said or did or thought or advised.

They were sitting in the back of a cab, hurtling down Eleventh Avenue over an old cobblestone section. Anne had managed it so that she was in the center between them. Ronald had the sense that she had wrapped her hand around Daphne's long and perfect inner thigh. But he could not see from where he was, and he felt inhibited about leaning forward and turning his head in that direction and looking.

Then he felt Anne's hand gently cup his genitals, and at the same time he felt the gentle circles of her warm breath on his neck as she commanded in his ear.

"Don't move. Relax. Let me enjoy you. I want to use you. Relax. Don't you want to please me? I promise you will like doing what I tell you to do. I know what pleases gay boys. You don't have to pretend you're bisexual with me. I know you." He shuddered and could not tell if it was from fear or excitement.

Ronald stood like a statue, as Anne had directed him to, one arm behind his head the other about to grip his cock, which was standing erect frozen stiff. He was unsure if he was really unable to move or just pretending.

Daphne lay across a long plush velvet couch, the kind Cleopatra is always shown reclining upon, on her back, arching her pelvis into the air. She was stiff and naked, propped on her elbows. Her snatch had been shaved smooth except for a dark stripe. She had the far-away look of someone in a yoga trance.

In heels, stockings, garter belt and bustier, all black, Anne bent down between Daphne's upraised parted legs and gently tongued her cunt, which was running moist with desire.

Ronald was excited and nervous. He was at the waxing salon. Anne had suggested it, and it became an irresistible compulsion to have his body smooth. All the hair on his body had just been removed. It made him see himself as he never had before when he looked in the three way mirror.

"What do you think?" Jimmi asked.

"I'm overwhelmed. Thank you."

Jimmi smiled.

"I can't believe it," Ronald said.

"That's the usual response the first time," Jimmi said. "And so is that," he added pointing to the outstretched cock hard as rock that grew as Ronald looked at himself. "Here, let me do one last thing. It's included in the price."

He dropped to his knees in front of Ronald, wrapped his arms around his smooth buns and took his hard cock in his mouth. Slowly at first, lipping only the crown, he started to bring Ronald to a frenzy. He took more of it in his mouth, going deeper and deeper until the head of Ronald's cock was pocketed in the depth of his throat and he was chewing on the rod without using his teeth.

Ronald's smooth and hairless body gleamed and glistened with the sweat that covered it. He began to caress his own nipples, moaning cries from the depth of his solar plexus until he found himself shattering in an explosion that sent him out beyond the boundaries of himself. He grabbed at Jimmi's hair, but the boy was entranced and kept on sucking him so tender now it almost ached. When he finally released him, Ronald raised the attendant and kissed him on the lips.

"Thank you," said Jimi.

"Thank you," said Ronald.

They showered and Jimi dried and oiled him.

Anne said you should wear these and be at her place at noon.

Everything was black, black leather shorts that demanded an exquisite body of whoever wore them, a ribbed, silk, form-fitting sleeveless muscle shirt, calf-high boots, a black leather bracelet with a watch face on his left wrist, a three banded silver ring on the middle finger of his left hand. All these things served to highlight the bronzed gleaming skin that he showed with pride.

Even on Christopher Street, where they had seen everything, heads turned as he passed on his way to Anne's loft on Hudson, oblivious to everything but the pride he took in his own surrender to her. She had dared him to be himself, and he felt free. His head was in the clouds.

Once again he was playing the statue at Anne's. Ronald's cold hard cock stood like an icicle in the air as he watched her tongue the cunt of the exquisite girl he had failed to love. He wore a black leather belt around his waist, a collar, and rings in his nipples.

Anne rose from the sacramental bowl of Daphne's lilacs, revitalized. "Come here," she ordered Ronald, and he approached. She took hold of him by his cold hard cock.

Ronald was stretched to immobility. His cock was an iron bar inside Daphne; his body was stiff and flat as a planed plank of oak suspended above her, His head was arched, thrown back; his body was supported by his open palms and steely toes pressed against the divan. His eyes were wide and staring into a void.

Daphne was just as stiff, her cunt thrust up to him, her inner walls clasping the pressure of his cock inside her. Her chest was taut, her breasts hard, her eyes focused on a blue spot of light on the ceiling in which she saw Anne's face, her tongue straining to penetrate the phantom lips.

Anne moaned with pleasure as she looked at the marvel she had wrought and exploded in cascading orgasms. "So much," she thought, "for heterosexuality."

Matthew held David's head between his hands and looked into his eyes lost in wonder and gratitude. The sable sand was soft beneath them. The sun beat down out of a cloudless, boundless blue sky.

The turquoise Caribbean, a sea that stretches from an infinite horizon, was coming to pieces in white flakes of foam at its edges. It broke against the beach and, rushing, hit the ragged surface of the black rock formation that stretched at broken intervals along the shore. At that same instant, when its waves slivered into shards of foam, the sea rebounded as so many rounds of spray shooting back into itself.

End of the 3ʳᵈ Book

THE FACE BENEATH THE MASK

GIDEON ELLIOT

The Face beneath the Mask

His voice was very near and very far away. "How much longer do you think you will find it interesting to cast yourself in this role?"

He pulled me, jerked me, really, to him by the leash that was attached to the collar I was wearing. I nearly stumbled, but with an exercise of foot work independent of thought, I managed to keep my balance and return to the rigid posture of attention I kept during these sessions. "Don't you ever get tired of it?" I was ashamed to say I didn't.

"No, sir," I said, my eyes cast down.

"I do," he said, "and I do not want to go on this way, and I won't." I stood entirely still, not moving a muscle. His distant beauty overwhelmed me. "It's not enough for me," he said. "I want a partner, not a slave. A slave," he repeated. "That's actually funny. Your absolute submission is a burden. You are using me, and I want it to stop, but you don't. Not only you don't, but you can't." I still did not stir, my eyes cast down. But I understood this was not the usual routine we'd go through of verbal abuse and humiliation.

"I'm not playing," he said. "Don't pretend I'm saying this to gratify your kinks. It's over. I don't want it. I want you out of here. And you don't need to keep your eyes lowered. It might do you good to look straight at me for once and see if you can see who I really am. Look at what you never even noticed me.

My body, my face, that's what you noticed; you noticed my looks and they fit, perfectly, into your fantasy. You turned me into an actor in your fantasy. I know; I let you. But no more. It seems I prefer reality. I want you out by Friday. You like orders. That's my final order. Your stuff, too. It's over."

There was nothing I could say. I was numb. I knew this was not in the script. He was not going to finish his admonition with a frightening whipping and soothing caresses when I finished crying. I absorbed his dismissal with the capitulation to inevitability that had become my second nature.

I sat at my desk Monday, neglecting my work, checking the real estate section with a sense of unreality. Mandy walked in with a coffee for me and one for him. "Looking for a job?" he joked, alluding to the company shake-up we both had recently survived, when he saw the newspaper on my desk, squashed up against the computer, open to the classified section.

"I'm looking for a place to live," I said.

"What happened? Are you ok?"

"Yeah, I'm alright. Nervous, but it'll be ok. Bobby wants me out."

"Stay at my place."

"What?"

"I mean it. You can stay at my place, as long as you need to."

"That's very kind of you."

"There's an empty bedroom."

"I know. How are you coping?"

"I'm ok."

I looked doubtful.

"Really, I am," he said. "I'm tougher than you, in general, emotionally." I looked at him doubtfully. "I really am ok. It's funny," he continued after we had both been silent. "It's funny how things should," he hesitated, searching for the words, "converge like this."

"You sure it's ok?" I said.

"Yes," he said quietly, "it is."

~~oOo~~

It was not difficult to live with Mandy. Unlike at the office, he was quiet and never expected anything of me more than the household agreements we drew up including what my share of expenses would be and which night I cooked and whose week was it to keep the bathroom clean, stuff like that. I felt like I had my own place.

"You can't let yourself go," Mandy said after it was noticeable that I had gained a few pounds. I sighed, ashamed. "I know," I said.

"What happened?" he asked, as if he didn't know.

"I lack discipline without him," I said.

"Discipline, I don't know about," Mandy said. "But I can provide structure."

He did. We set up a space in the basement, got some weights and a chinning bar, and worked out at least an hour a day, during the week, in the evening, after we got home. We'd take some high protein shakes and vitamins and nuts and berries, have a shower, and then spend an hour in our basement gym. We showered again afterwards. On weekends we sometimes spent hours on end working out, salting a few household tasks, like shopping for the week's food or doing repairs around the house, in between.

We were good together. But all that time we were so bodily present to each other and naked together in the shower where we even washed each other's backs and complimented each other's hardons, we never did anything more. There was no embarrassment. We'd come, I don't know how, to an agreement that we would not go there, even though I had no doubt he found me attractive, and I knew he knew I found him wonderfully alluring. It was part of the discipline. It gave substance to the structure.

"You look great," I said, soaping his arms as well as his back.

"So do you," he said turning around, tousling my wet hair.

We wrestled in the shower a little, soapy skin sliding over soapy skin, but we left it at that, dried each other off, slipped on identical silky black mini-boxers and prepared tea in the kitchen and sat at the counter on stools facing each other and sipping it hot excited by our hard, cold, locked-up arousal. We lived inside a ritual rather than in a relationship. It was as near perfection as I have ever been. But I had to lose it to know that.

"You talk too much." It was not hostile. Sam Bernstein, I was to learn, was like that. He said what he thought, without thinking. He first came up to me at a filmmakers' party in TriBeCa that Mandy took me to. That's where I met him. It was early June and we were standing on the roof with champagne flutes filled with Bollinger, and looking at the Empire State Building. He was right. I was nervous. I felt like I was on display and not up to the standard I saw all around me.

"It won't be there much longer," a lean man with a perfectly-groomed beard standing near us said. "You'll see. If the terrorists don't get it, the real estate developers will."

"Cut the shit," a bullet headed bald fellow, a would be dom, obviously drunk, wearing a Hawaiian shirt, cargo shorts, and flip flops said in response.

I felt a strong, gentle hand take me by the shoulder. I turned and saw a man whose eyes were alive with the awareness of his power. There was determination in the set of his jaw. His face radiated intense masculine beauty. Sam was, is, exquisite: high cheekbones, dark blue eyes, thick brown hair, rich cupid's bow lips, a commanding jaw, grace, and a lithe muscular build that just came with the body.

"Do you mind, Mandy?" he asked graciously as he pulled me to him.

"Of course not, Sam," Mandy said, "but maybe I should introduce you first."

"Don't bother," Sam said touching the air with his palm and smiling. "I think I know how to introduce myself." He shepherded me off the terrace – I did not resist -- into a library with an old inlaid, mahogany writing desk, several brown leather easy chairs, a matching sofa, and gilt-framed pictures on the walls, or at least on the walls that were not covered with shelves of books.

Several brass candelabras wired for low watt amber bulbs were placed glowing around the room. He closed the door behind us. He smiled and took me in his arms. "You are very beautiful," he said. "You are irresistible." He kissed me. I opened to him and felt his breath fill me. I blazed and became the flame that extinguished me.

~~oOo~~

The next morning we walked along the paths in Central Park.

"You want someone to tell you what to do," Sam said. I looked at him and smiled. "What?"

"Don't be vulgar. You heard me."

"I don't know what to say," I said.

"Exactly what I mean," he said, nodding his head at the confirmation of his analysis. "I'll tell you what to say. Say what it is you want. You send out very confusing signals." I shrugged. "I don't want anything," I said.

"Right," he said. "What else?" I was entirely stymied. "There's nothing else," I said.

"I like empty-headed men," he said, taking me gently and firmly by the back of my neck. "It's so easy to make them do what I want," he added gazing at me with the most bedroom eyes I have ever seen. "Don't you want to do what I want?" he said but only with his eyes.

I nodded agreement only with mine as his lips touched mine, and his breath enveloped mine, and everything became his. I'd been, as it were, tossed out the window, but now, cat-like, I'd landed on all fours. Everything was different and nothing had changed.

When I told Mandy I was going to move in with Sam, he said he was not surprised but wished I'd give it a second thought. I told him there really was nothing to think about: I felt drawn to Sam in a way I had never felt drawn to anyone before.

"Are you sure of that?"

"What are you suggesting?" I answered.

"I'm not suggesting anything except that you be cautious before you do anything you are going to wish you had not done."

"This is too complicated for me," I said smiling. "Are you saying this because you are jealous," It was an offensive thing to say, especially to him. He smiled and extended his hand. "I'll miss the work-outs," he said.

"We'll still get to do them sometimes," I said.

"No," he said. "You'll see. I'm not complaining, and I'm not jealous. I'm saying what I know. It's ok. I'm always here."

You can imagine what I was imagining it would be like to live with Sam, to look at him always and always to be near him and able to touch him. The erotic resonance of being shaped to perfection, moreover, through compliance to such a Master's discipline, the frisson of obedience, the statuesque periods of frozen posing during which my whole body throbbed with the vibrancy of an erection, all that and more tormented my imagine with impatience.

But there was none of that. It began promisingly enough when he ordered me to strip. But nothing happened after I complied. My daily routine entailed domestic service: performing menial household tasks, doing the laundry, running errands, dusting and vacuuming. But he did not eroticize it in the least, the days to come came to show.

Our first night, after a day I had not been let into his presence, he ordered me to strip. I 'anticipated it would begin. He led me naked to my room. He held the door for me. I entered, but when I stepped aside once I was inside, to let him in, instead he closed the door from outside without saying a word and I was locked in by myself anticipating he would return but not knowing what was going to happen next. When nothing happened, apprehension gave way to boredom and petulance.

Sam was nowhere to be seen, in the morning, when I was brought a cup of coffee by the cook, a tight-lipped man in his sixties. He sat with me while I drank it, as if aware of my impotent fury and to make sure I kept it contained. I went about the day's tasks, as he directed me, and did not see Sam that evening either, nor for another two weeks, and then only fleetingly.

I was ordered to put on jeans and a t-shirt and pick up his dinner jacket at the dry cleaners. It was not Sam who sent me. Mr. Horely, the cook did, but I caught a glimpse of Sam as I lingered in the hall outside his dressing room. I saw his magnificent physique, a snowy, white towel hitched below his waist, reflected through the doorway from inside the room onto one of the grand mirrors in the hall.

Then the door closed and I went back to my room, stripped, and since I had nothing to do and nothing, as far as I was beginning to be able to tell, to look forward to, I lay down on the narrow bed that was in my cell. I was waiting, but no longer waiting for him. I was just waiting for this to end, for something to change, even if it was only for the change that happens when you fall asleep.

The End

Here is a sample from another story you may enjoy:

5-BOOK BOX SET

Blue
Identity

Gay Erotic Romance
GIDEON ELLIOT

There was nothing more I could do. He was gone and I knew there was no way I could bring him back. Perhaps that was a good thing. Perhaps it wasn't.

What I could do was take a shower, scrub myself down, shave, get dressed, go out and get a haircut, buy some new clothes, work out at the gym, go for a drink at Benny's, stop in at the new sushi place on Barrow Street, get home around midnight, get stoned, listen to Jauchtzet Gott in Allen Landen, the Schwarzkopf recording, jerk off, and get some sleep. Tomorrow morning I'd go into work.

It would keep me busy. It would keep me going. And that's really all that mattered after all.

* * *

Ellen was waiting for me on the doorstep when I got home.

"You look better than I expected," she said.

"What did you expect?"

"A wreck," she said.

"Sorry to disappoint you," I said.

"I'm not disappointed," she said. "I'm glad. Anybody after almost ten years..."

"What are you doing?" I said, quietly.

"What do you mean?"

"You know perfectly well what I mean."

It never failed. She was getting me angry. The last thing I needed. It was a trick of hers. But I caught myself in time.

"I don't want to do this, Ellen," I said with no affect.

"You don't want to do what?" she said.

She was baiting the hook. She'd use any response as a way into a fight. Fighting was foreplay for her. I wasn't having it, and I wasn't going to explain. Even that was a way of involving me. I wasn't even going to explain why I wasn't going to explain.

"Good night, Ellen," I said unlocking the door to the building.

"You don't know what's good for you," she said, on the verge of crying.

It wasn't going to work.

"Perhaps," I said. "But I'll deal with it. Good night." I let myself in and disappeared behind the door, closing it gently behind me, leaving her there.

Actually, I felt better than I thought I would.

If you enjoyed this sample then look for **Blue Identity**.

Also by this Author

A Second Chance

The Recruiter

A Furtive and Hidden Embrace

Diamond Shadows

Displacement

Keen Obedience

Between Two Thieves

Heart's Desire

Sensual Surrender

Erotic Aggression

Don't Forget You Love Me

Unstable Emotion

The Hazard Game

A Knight in the Forest

Captured Emotions

The Mesmerist's Tale

On His Own

The Good Bitch

Succumb Touch

Blue Identity

My Fair Master

Carnal Spellbound

Sweet Surrender

Hypnotized

Slaves of Sex

Decisions

***

I REALLY LOVE Reviews!

If you enjoyed this book, please share the love and don't forget to leave a review on Amazon or the site of any other retailer you purchased this book from!

I highly appreciate your reviews, and it only takes a minute to write & post one. I can't tell you how much this means to me!

You'll find the list of all my books on my Author Central page... just in case you'd like to leave a review for other books of mine you've read but didn't have time to leave a review.

Amazon Author Central – http://www.amazon.com/Gideon-Elliot/e/B00DUYBEQC

One Last Thing, For Kindle Readers...

When you turn the page, Kindle will give you the opportunity to rate this book and share your thoughts on Facebook and Twitter. If you enjoyed my writings, would you please take a few seconds to let your friends know about it? Because... when they enjoy they will be grateful to you and so will I.

Thank You!

Gideon Elliot
gideon_elliot@awesomeauthors.org

About the Author

Gideon Elliot was born in 1981 in Wichita, Kansas.

He grew up in San Francisco and spends the greater part of the year, now, on one of the Cyclades Islands in Greece where he runs a jazz café, paints, writes poetry, and swims.

He has a small apartment in Greenwich Village, where he stays from the middle of November to the end of April and, during those months, manages an erotic men's clothing shop. He began writing erotic fiction at the age of fifteen.

You may also like the books by these authors:

A TRADE FOR A TRADE
GAY ROMANCE EROTICA

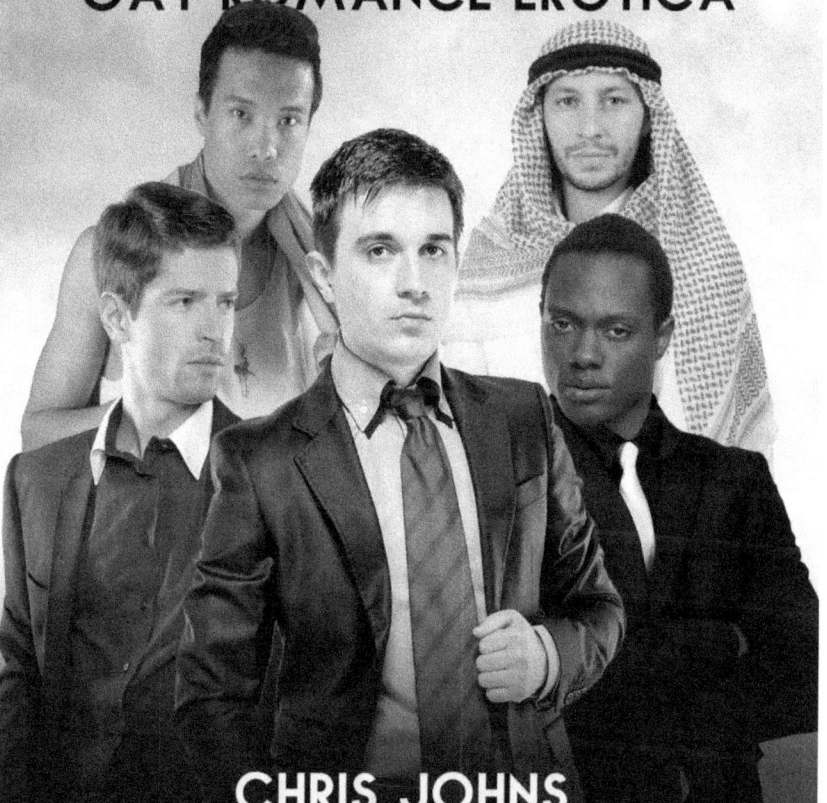

CHRIS JOHNS

The only word I could think of as I looked at the training room and the trading floor next to it was, 'intimidating.' Today was the day I was going to start changing my life, and this is where I was going to start.

It all started about a week ago. On the underground going to work in my dead end job, I picked up a financial paper left by a previous traveller and started reading it. 'Become a Forex Trader,' an advert at the back said. It gave a website to go to for more information, so I tore the ad out and put it in my pocket. That night I read all the blurb on the web, it sounded fantastic. I booked there and then for a seminar to lay out how I was going to develop the skills to earn a six-figure income in less than three years. The day of the seminar, I called in sick and went. Wow, what they showed us was amazing. The only problem was, it would take all my savings to buy the training.

At 20 years old, with a couple of decent A levels and not much else, I was never going to get a well-paid job unless I took a chance on something that could jump me out of my miserable existence. I handed over my credit card and saw my miserably small life savings disappear.

So, here I was in this amazing place, with little more than a determination to get through the next few days. While I waited for everyone else to arrive, I took in my surroundings and the people that populated it. The reception area was very plush with high tables and stools, a kitchenette with endless supplies of coffee, chocolate and tea. The trading floor was a mass of computer screens with loads of men and women working them, but all seemingly very laid back. I was looking at it through a glass wall. Next to it was the training room, also with a glass wall, it looked high-tech, which I found out very quickly was the case.

A few of the people who worked there looked to be in their 50s, a larger number in their 30s and three who only looked a few years older than me. All three of them were dressed to kill. I scoped them out thoroughly, hoping they had not seen where my eyes went. They looked good enough to eat and my cock stirred at the thought of getting at their bodies.

I had time for a coffee before we were ushered into the training room. The guy who stood to the lectern at the side of the giant screen was the dishiest of the three young guys. He was what I would call chunky. Not slim, but definitely not fat either. He was wearing a button down dress shirt, open at the collar. His designer jeans looked expensive and looked as though these, along with the shirt, had been moulded for his body. Great pecs and a juicy looking bulge at the crotch had me fully erect. I just had to hope I wouldn't be asked to stand up because there was no way my more than adequate man meat was not going to be noticed.

His name was Andy and during the course of the morning session, we found out he had come here straight from university three years ago, so, 24, I guessed. He now traded a personal six-figure account and a seven-figure one for a client. He traded once per day and when he wasn't lecturing, he lived in Ko Samui in Thailand with his Californian partner. It was some time before I found out that partner was same sex.

After the first session, the lecturer was the second one of the young guys. He was black, over six feet tall and well-built. I guessed his suit would have cost upwards to £750. Shirt and tie were great, completed with a pair of obviously hand-tooled leather shoes. He looked like a model for Saville Row Tailor. He delivered a psychology lecture as smooth as his looks and dress. He was almost as stunning as Andy and introduced himself as Lee, a couple of years older than Andy and already a senior trader. Like many of his race, he looked younger than his 26. Trousers tailored so that nothing of his manhood showed, but he was sexy.

Lunch was a buffet and meant to impress, it was superb.

After lunch we had the third of the young guns. His name was Durgas, 29, and a Sikh. He was imposing. He wore a black turban, skin tight black T shirt, skin tight black designer jeans and patent leather shoes. Not much left to the imagination front or back.

All three of these guys had gorgeous arses, and Andy and Durgas had interesting bulges. I assumed that Lee would be the biggest because of his race. All three were fantastically good looking and spoke beautifully. I hoped in three years' time, I would look as good; the basics were there, I just needed the money to make it look as good.

I'm sure I made a fool of myself because for two days, I asked a gazillion questions and no one else seemed to ask any at all. End of the course and Lee approached me.

"Alan, I've been seriously impressed with your enthusiasm, so, I'm taking you as my student for your trading floor course. We'll be one to one for all the future sessions spread over the next few weeks. You have your trading account set up and funded, you have your trading platform, so go away and start trading. Remember your risk management, call the graduate line any time you have a query and I'll see you back here on Monday at 0900. We'll analyse your trades and spend the day together on the floor looking at more advanced methods of keeping the good ones going and leaving the bad ones behind."

I wondered what was going on. We were only allocated three sessions, not all day. Was I receiving special treatment for some reason?

If you enjoyed this sample then look for <u>A Trade For A Trade</u>.

OWNED
in SINGAPORE

GAY SUBMISSION EROTICA

DEXTER CHASE

"Alex, come in, sit down. Coffee?"

Alexander Dupree did as he was told and thanked his boss. "Black with two, please, Sir."

He was very wary as to why he was being talked to in such a friendly manner. His performance to date had earned him two warning letters. The next time it would be dismissal, and the last thing Alex could afford at the present time was the sack.

"I'm sure you are aware that your performance this year has been well below what we have come to expect from you. Two years ago you were on track to make partner. Then, a little less than a year ago it all started to unravel for you. We have been very disappointed because we saw you as the future. You were our senior associate, and the youngest. I have talked to the other partners and we have made a decision concerning your future."

Alex took the coffee offered to him as his boss spoke. Was this the big push being built up to by giving him all the reasons for it? He knew he had been underperforming. During his first two years with the partnership he had closed so many difficult deals he had become something of a legend. He was only 26, single and considered a premium catch for any female. His apartment in the centre of town was furnished in the height of good taste and luxury, his BMW convertible was less than two years old. His level of debt was frightening.

The boss sat back down behind his desk and looked hard at his fallen star.

"I am sure you are aware that our best efforts to secure the deal with Straits Technical have not borne fruit. We think that in your hay day you would have tied this up with little effort so we are giving you a last chance to prove yourself. We are sending you to Singapore to replace Jason Oakley on the negotiating team. He will remain to assist you, but this will be your deal to make or lose. If you bring the deal back we will tear up your two written warnings, re-instate you as senior associate and guarantee you a partnership in twelve months if you then continue to perform the way you did before the drop in standards."

Alex knew he could do it if he could just get over his feeling of loss at his poor performance. He had no idea why he had lost it, but after the first written warning he got depressed and his underperformance accelerated. If he could start again he knew he would be ok. The pressure to succeed where everyone else had failed just acted as a challenge to him now.

"Thank you, Sir. I won't let you down."

"We hope not, Alex. We don't want to lose you but we need results to be better than your last year has produced."

Coffee finished, detailed folder presented to him.

"Take that away and absorb it. Be ready to leave for Singapore after the weekend."

That was it. Alex spent the weekend absorbing the contents of the folder. He spoke to Jason Oakley for hours getting all the personal details of the negotiating team from Singapore Technical. It was his ability to get the opposing negotiating teams onside that had been his greatest asset, now he needed it again, big time.

Monday morning, a first class seat on Singapore Airways and he was on his way. He was so pleased he could link his laptop to a power source because virtually the whole of the flight he was working on it. Jason met him at Changi and whisked him away to his hotel.

"We are going in for another round of talks after lunch, Alex. Do you want to sit in or have a rest and start fresh tomorrow?"

"I'll sit in, Jason. Introduce me to the other team and I'll just observe today. Conference with our team tonight and then I'll take over tomorrow morning."

Jason had mixed feelings being replaced by this much younger man who he knew had failed to shine the last twelve months.

"Very well, Alex. I'll give you all the support I can, but believe me, you will need a miracle to get Phillip Chen to go down our road in this deal."

"But he is only one man, what about the others?"

"The others are lackeys. They just say what Phillip tells them to. If you crack him you have the deal, but none of us have been able to."

During the afternoon sitting, Alex observed Phillip Chen closely, not missed by Phillip himself. Phillip had noticed Alex for different reasons to what should have been expected.

By the time Alex went to bed that night, despite the 8 hour time zone change, he slept like a baby, completely wiped out, but confident he had a handle on this whole deal, ready to do battle.

If you enjoyed this sample then look for <u>Owned In Singapore</u>.

Chatting for TOKENS

HOT GAY ROMANCE EROTICA

DICK PARKER

I hate to admit it but I was surfing online for some porn. Yeah, I know, that seems kind of creepy but I was horny and wanted to watch something to jack off. Most of the sites I looked at were guys that were too old or too much like biker guys. I like slim young guys like myself.

I stumbled onto a site called Chat and Jack. I wondered what it was and clicked on it. The site opened and there was a menu of what I could choose to see. There were Women, Men, Couples, and Groups. I clicked on Men.

The window opened and there were about fifty small screens with guys on them. Some were naked, some were clothed and some were in between. I looked through them and many were older guys but there were some young hot guys too. I found one that was shirtless and in his boxers. It was pretty obvious he had a boner. I clicked on his little box.

The site opened with a screen where I had to fill in a user name and password. I hesitated but then looked and didn't see anywhere where I had to put in a credit card, so I made up a password and user name. Then the screen opened and there was the guy and by now he had his boxers off. Damn he had a big cut cock and he was stroking it.

On the side of the screen a chat was going on. I read and watched the guy. He had a microphone and was talking to the chat people.

Then there was a chime sound and someone tipped him 25 tokens. He thanked them and bent over and pulled his butt cheeks apart and showed his butt hole. Damn!

My dick was hard by now and I pulled down my pants and played with it. The kid was really cute and well built. I watched the chat and figured it out. Guys asked for him to do stuff and if they tipped him, he did it.

I didn't know how they got the tokens to tip but I was pretty interested in watching him. He had a nice dick. It was probably a bit over six inches and thick. He was shaved and so was his asshole.

Soon he said for 200 tokens he'd put a dildo in his butt. He held up a big black dildo and the tips began coming in. Some tipped 10 tokens and other tipped 25. One guy tipped 100 tokens. It didn't take long and he had the dildo in his butt.

I was really hard and jacking. Many of the chatters were also jacking, or so they said. I looked at the top of the screen and saw there were 483 viewers. Wow, that was hot. He had over four hundred guys watching him. That turned me on.

I was jerking my dick and wondered how many of the 400 others were doing that. It made me really horny thinking of so many guys watching and getting off.

The kid had the dildo in his ass and he put up on the screen that when they hit his goal of 500 more tokens, he would cum in his mouth. The screen lit up with guys tipping tokens. It only took a couple of minutes and they got to 500. Then he lay on his back with the dildo in his ass yet and flipped up his legs and began jacking off with his dick over his face.

I lay back in my chair and stroked myself and watched him. I was close so I slowed down and edged myself hoping to cum when he did. It took a few minutes but then he said he was going to cum. I sped up and I came just before he squirted all over his face and into his open mouth. My belly was covered with cum and I was exhausted. It was the horniest cum I'd had in a long time.

The kid wiped up and thanked the tippers and then he was gone. I went back to the menu and picked another to watch. This one only had 45 viewers. His name was Derrick and he was a cutie. I decided to try chatting so I typed 'Hi good looking', and hit send.

He was reading the posts and had on a tee shirt and boxers. He didn't have a microphone apparently because there was no sound. He typed back, 'Hi Rascal, thnx'.

Damn, he answered me. He looked about my age, 20, and was really cute. The others weren't chatting very much so I thought I'd try to talk to him.

'How long you been doing this?'

'About 6 months."

'My first time on site.'

'Thanks for viewing me.'

'How do you get online like you are?'

"See button…BROADCAST?'

I looked. I saw the button.

'Go there. You have to fill out age form. Show proof of 18. Then turn on cam.'

'What you do with tokens?'

'I get 5 cents for each. They pay every month.'

'Make a lot?'

'If you're cute and have a big dick.'

'LOL'

He smiled at the cam. I liked this guy. He was really cute and seemed like a nice guy. He was quite tall and skinny with brown curly hair and hazel eyes.

'You going to try it?'

'I might.'

'Kind of scary the first time but it's fun.'

'It turns me on to know guys watching.'

He grinned and nodded. Then he pulled down the front of his boxers and showed me his cock. Damn he had a nice long cut dick with a big mushroom head.

'Nice,' I typed.

Just then someone tipped 50 tokens. Then another tipped 25.

The kid thanked them and took off his shirt. He was skinny but had a nice chest and perky little nipples.

'Hey Rascal, look on the lower right and click on FOLLOW. That way when I come on to cam you'll get an email.'

I clicked on it.

'I did it.'

He grinned into the cam. Then he typed. '100 more tokens and I'll cum.'

The tokens came flying in. In no time he had nearly 200.

Then he slowly pulled his boxers down and turned around so we could see his ass. Oh man he had a beautiful ass. My cock was hard as hell again and I began jacking it.

Derrick knelt on his bed and began jacking himself. His balls were low hangers and they swung back and forth as he jerked his cock. He ran his hand down his chest and played with his balls.

I looked at his big cock and stroked mine. I'd just cum but I was very hard again. I noticed the viewers box was growing. He had over a hundred viewers now. He turned around and bent over and pulled his ass cheeks apart and showed us his hole. Oh man.

The viewer box said 254 now. He lay back and arched up his back and squirted cum up onto his chest and chin. I jacked furiously and came for a second time.

Derrick lay there grinning and then he took his finger and scooped up some cum and ate it. Tokens came in like a snowstorm.

He picked up his boxers and wiped himself up.

'Nice.' I typed.

He saw my message and winked at me. Damn I think he liked me. Then I noticed a PVT message on the screen. I didn't know what it was and finally I saw a box and clicked on it.

"My email is: Derrickdanger@hotmail.com. Email me."

Damn he gave me his email. He waved goodbye and was gone.
I sat there for a minute. This was a horny site and it turned me on to watch these guys. I wondered where Derrick lived. He was probably in some place thousands of miles away.

I went back to the computer and clicked on the BROADCAST page and filled out the forms. I scanned my driver's license and sent it. The message said they'd verify me in 24 hours.

I opened my email. Should I mail him or just let it go? What the hell?

I emailed him. "Hi Derrick, I really enjoyed watching you. That was very hot. I don't know if I'm good looking enough to broadcast but it sure turns me on to think about it. Where do you live? I mean what state? I really think you're very cute and would like to get to know you with emails. Well anyway, thanks for the show. Rascal."

He'd get my email when I sent it. I hesitated and then hit send.

If you enjoyed this sample then look for **Chatting For Tokens.**

AMY REDEK

His
SPECIAL
LESSONS

Quentin College was a place that I had taken a fancy to when I was studying for my doctorate at University and was very pleased when I received a letter asking me to attend an interview. I was one of twenty there that day and I progressed into the next interview of ten and finally for a third visit of just three of us for a position in such a prestigious college.

I was the last to be interviewed and I went into the Dean's office to find two other people sitting there along with the Dean himself, who had been present at my two previous visits. He was sitting behind his large desk and flanked by a man on his right and a woman on his left. I knew of them through my studies and the newspapers but waited until I was formally introduced to them before speaking.

'Sit down, Dr. Smith,' Dean Ainsworth said, indicating the chair placed before the desk. 'I am pleased to see that you made it to the last three and through your work, I'm sure you know Mrs. Cynthia Carrington who is attached to the Department of Education in the present government.' I nodded in her direction and gave her a small smile. 'And Sir Reginald Hudson, who, though in opposition at the moment, is the Chairman of the College Board of Governors.' I nodded in his direction and gave him the same smile.

'To recap for their benefit, you were born on the 14th May 1974 in London, christened Colin Franklin Smith and are now twenty-six years of age with both parents now deceased. You won high honours at college and obtained your doctorate at Oxford in the field of Political History on a brilliant thesis showing the parallels between the English Civil War and the American war of Independence. You have also written a book using these lines, which I myself have read and have ordered copies for the college library.

Now having seen you twice previously, I'll let my esteemed colleagues put forward their questions as to why you think you are fit for the position in this college. Mrs. Carrington, if you would be so kind as to lead off.'

He sat back with a smile on his face and listened to the questions that were fired at me for over half an hour and to my answers. They were very demanding and I gave the best answers that I could and felt mentally drained when it was over and shook hands all round before I left, being told that I would be notified within a week if I'd succeeded to the post or not.

I went back to London to my home in Chelsea. A house in Cheyne Walk left to me by my parents two years ago. My father had been a cardiac consultant, but his profession did nothing for him for he died of a heart attack at the age of sixty-one. Mother, with his loss, just seemed to pine away and so followed him two years later, but it was recorded as natural causes in her case.

That was two and a half years ago and so I went off to America to further my education in my field and had only been back in England for three months before applying for this doctorate post of Political History at Quentin College. In the States, I had attended Yale University, and by having the other side of the story as it were about what led up to the War of Independence, prompted me to write my thesis.

True to their word, I received a letter a week after my last interview from Dean Ainsworth congratulating me on securing the post and could take up residence whenever I wished for the incumbent had already retired. It was two weeks into the summer holidays and another four weeks before the new term year began; and as I didn't have any ties, immediately packed all that I would need and set off for the college.

Before the taxi driver could even begin to grumble about helping me get my two trunks down to his cab, I gave him a fiver and then had him drive me to the station where I had to get a porter to get them to my platform. The train I wanted was there and people were already boarding and I just had enough time to get my ticket and see the trunks put into the guards van.

If you enjoyed this sample then look for **His Special Lessons**.

4FUN PUBLISHING

ULTIMATE SUPER MEGA BUNDLE (30M/M BOOK BOX SET)

30 SHADES of GAY

BEST GAY STORIES OF 2015

Best Gay Stories of 2015 by three bestselling authors - Chris Johns, Gideon Elliot and Hank Brooks!

Things aren't always black and white. In gay love, there are various shades – sweet romance, erotic romance, there's domination and submission, interracial and inter-generational love stories, mystery, and just pure gay sex.

30 Shades of Gay is full of erotic male on male action that is so intense they fall on moral "gray areas".

30 M/M Super Mega Bundle gives you:
Border Patrol by Chris Johns
My Street Urchin by Chris Johns
Foreign Seduction by Chris Johns
Heart's Desire by Gideon Elliot
Unstable Emotion by Gideon Elliot
Erotic Aggression by Gideon Elliot
A Second Chance by Gideon Elliot
Sensual Surrender by Gideon Elliot
Forgiven by Hank Brooks
Divine Guilt by Hank Brooks
As You Are by Hank Brooks
Blood Work by Hank Brooks
Body Sweat by Hank Brooks
Harry's Trial by Hank Brooks
Fantasy Play by Hank Brooks
Secret Desire by Hank Brooks
Horny Visitors by Hank Brooks
Doubtful Heart by Hank Brooks
Pleasure Thirst by Hank Brooks
Fountain of Dreams by Hank Brooks
Year-Ender Surprise by Hank Brooks
Love Me If You Can by Hank Brooks
A Road To Nowhere by Hank Brooks

A Comfortable Sorrow by Hank Brooks
Elmwood Lane Secrets by Hank Brooks
Sensual Bet Rendezvous by Hank Brooks
A Commuter's Obsession by Hank Brooks
The Second Time Around by Hank Brooks
Another Chance of Delight by Hank Brooks
Backdoor Getaway Romance by Hank Brooks

If you enjoyed this sample then look for [30 Shades Of Gay](#).

WANT FREE COPIES OF MY BOOKS?
Just visit my blog and download free copies of my books:
http://gideon-elliot.awesomeauthors.org/gideon-elliot/